Rookie reader®

LIGHTNING LIZ

by Larry Dane Brimner

illustrated by Brian Floca

Children's Press®
A Division of Grolier Publishing
New York • London • Hong Kong • Sydney • Danbury, Connecticut

For E. Russell Primm III
— L. D. B.

Again, for Elizabeth (of course!)
— B. F.

Reading Consultant
Linda Cornwell
Learning Resource Consultant
Indiana Department of Education

Visit Children's Press® on the Internet at:
http://publishing.grolier.com

Library of Congress Cataloging-in-Publication Data
Brimner, Larry Dane.
Lightning Liz / by Larry Dane Brimner; illustrated by Brian Floca.
p. cm. — (A rookie reader)
Summary: An energetic young girl rushes on the way to bake a cake.
ISBN 0-516-20753-9 (lib. bdg.)   0-516-26360-9 (pbk.)
[1. Speed—Fiction.] I. Floca, Brian, ill. II. Title. III. Series.
PZ7.B767Li 1998
sq] —dc21
                              97-13835
                                 CIP
                                 AC

Liz is a flash of lightning.

No matter where she goes.
No matter how.

Liz goes in a hurry.

Through the park.

By the school.

On her skates.

On her scooter.

15

Uphill.

Downhill.

Frontwards . . .

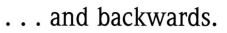

. . . and backwards.

Liz races.

And speeds.

And dashes and darts.

Here and there.

Everywhere.

What would you call
this flash of lightning?

Lightning Liz, of course!

About the Author

Larry Dane Brimner writes on a wide range of topics, from picture book and middle-grade fiction to young adult nonfiction. His previous Rookie Readers are *Brave Mary, How Many Ants?*, and *Firehouse Sal.* Mr. Brimner is also the author of *E-mail* and *The World Wide Web* for Children's Press and the award-winning *Merry Christmas, Old Armadillo* (Boyds Mills Press). He lives in the southwest region of the United States.

About the Illustrator

Brian Floca is the author and illustrator of *The Frightful Story of Harry Walfish* and the illustrator of several other books, among them *Poppy*, by Avi (winner of the 1996 *Boston Globe-Horn Book Award* for fiction), *Jenius: The Amazing Guinea Pig*, by Dick King-Smith, and *Luck with Potatoes*, by Helen Ketteman (a *Boston Globe* "best of '95" children's book). Brian Floca grew up in Temple, Texas, and currently lives near Boston, Massachusetts.